Javians
The Magnetisation of Java

BY
ARMAAN BHIMANI

ACKNOWLEDGMENTS

Special Thanks to

My dearest sister Arzoo
&
My Family

AUTHOR'S NOTE

This book has been divided into two journeys.

The first journey revolves around the magnetisation of Java whereas the second one talks about the singer of marshmallows!

I hope you get immersed into the world of Zephyr Village

- Armaan Bhimani

Head Leader Of Zephyr Village

Contents

PRELUDE	1
ROBERT'S HOME	3
THE CELESTIAL BUILDING	7
THE SPIRIT OF ZINC	11
LIGHTBUSTER!	14
THE HIDDEN PROPHECY	17
THE GENIE OF KRIULEM	20
THE CITY	24
THE ARMY OF DESERTHOLDERS	29
THE MONSTERS OF 3 DOORS	31
THE CUP OF JAVA	34
THE SHIP	38
MAGNETISATION OF JAVA	41
THE CURE	47
A ZEPHIRITE LIE	50
HAPPY BIRTHDAY ROBERT	53
TRAVELLING TO THE CAVES	55
THE RETURN OF LIGHTBUSTER	59
THE EVIL REQUEST	61
THE RUNAWAY THREE	64
THE DEMISE	67
WELCOME BACK	70
THE 16 TRAPDOORS	72

BLOOD AFTER BLOOD	75
SIDEQUEST!!!	79
EXTINCTION	82
THE RED BOLTER	84
THE LAST MARSHMALLOW	86
QUESTERMOLOGY	90
INTRODUCTION TO DRACULA	92
EPILOGUE	95
MAP	100

PRELUDE

A 10-year old boy named Robert finds a mysterious trapdoor and falls into a magical world called Zephyr Village.

Robert travels through a number of adventurous journeys in a quest to save the village from the clutches of several monsters called desertholders.

Intrigued with curiosity and a firm objective in mind to save the villagers, Robert uncovers several mysterious creatures that transforms him from one journey to another revealing many surprises in the voyage! Will Robert succeed?

Read on to find out.........

ROBERT'S HOME

A boy named Robert lived in Xyoster city. He was 10 years old. His home also included a science laboratory.

One day, he got a mark on his door. So, he went to a learned scientist named Oscar.

Oscar told him, "It must be the mark of invaders of the desertholders." Robert did not understand the revelation. He went back to his home. Robert went to sleep at midnight. He was trying to find out exactly who sent the mark.

On February 28 XY75, the truth became clear. As he was working on the mark, he noticed some scratches near his computer. He took a magnifying glass to find the source of the scratches. He followed the scratches until he reached a trapdoor. Robert had never seen the trapdoor located in his house. He said, "This trapdoor might lead to a new world unknown to me." He cleaned the dust from over the trapdoor.

The words on the trapdoor were etched in yellow ink which read as 'ZEPHYR VILLAGE'.

Robert was shocked and excited too. He wondered whether he should go or not. In a brief second, he made his choice. Robert tried opening the trapdoor. It was latched. Suddenly, a loud rap came, resulting in the trapdoor getting knocked off its hinges.

He stepped in the trapdoor. It was full of snow. Robert noticed more marks in the snow, similar to the ones he had found in his laboratory. He followed them. The marks stopped in front of a celestial big brown building.

THE CELESTIAL BUILDING

Robert wanted to find out who gave him the mark. So, he entered the building. A boy of age 12 was bound on the ground with ropes.

Robert cried, "Oh no! Who did this?"

He loosened the ropes and let the boy free, who thanked him.

The boy said, "It was the invaders of desertholders. They are a part of the desertholders' tyranny. One of those invaders from the team is living in this building. Take this sword, it will help you. It is dangerous to go unarmed."

"Thanks, friend", Robert said. He took the sword and went ahead.

After a while, Robert reached the 'Caves of Doom'. In this place, someone was dancing and singing. He turned to face Robert and said, "So you found the entrance to our world, young one? " It was Oscar.

Robert asked, "Who are you?"

"Who am I, but a desertholder." Saying this he turned into a dirty big brown beetle.

Oscar said, "I was the desertholder who left the marks and scratches near your computer."

Robert said, "You are a betrayer, Oscar."

"Yes! Enough talking now, time for you to die.", said Oscar.

He took out two blades and threw them at Robert, who defended himself with his sword. The blades shattered. Robert threw his sword at Oscar's face.

He dissolved, screeching, "No! No!"

Too late, the desertholder turned into a mist which said, "Go and find who is the thief of Zephyr village. Find him by June 3rd!"

THE SPIRIT OF ZINC

Robert turned behind and ran out of the cave. The boy who gave him the sword said," Run, Robert! I hope you got the task?"

Robert said, "Yes!"

The boy said, "I am Longerst and I will accompany you on your journey."

Robert asked, "How did the trapdoor come into my house?"

Longerst said, "Ten children have the trapdoor. They are lost in my world. Oscar fought them and won, but you survived."

They started walking. There was a big avalanche nearing them. Robert tripped in the snow and broke his tooth. A smooth mixture of zinc and mist had hit him.

Longerst cried," That is the spirit of zinc. Get up, Robert!"

Before Robert could get up, there was an attack from under the snow that hit Robert. The spirit of zinc got up, taking two blades from inside his zinc armor, and threw them at Longerst and Robert. They were zinc ropes, not blades.

The spirit of zinc said, "Time for you to die."

But, before it could do anything, a silver beam of light hit it on the chest and it collapsed. Immediately, the avalanche stopped.

LIGHTBUSTER!

Robert stood transfixed, staring at the spot the spirit had collapsed. Another beam of light shot from behind, turning the spirit into a zinc sword. The ropes broke on their own.

"That is for you, little scientist", said a voice. "I am Lightbuster. I am 14 and I live in the Valley Of Zinc. I saw that you needed my help and so arrived at your help."

Robert took the sword. Now, he had two swords. Lightbuster

already knew Longerst. It turned out, they were old friends.

Lightbuster was in the lead and Longerst and Robert were following him.

"Where is this thief, anyway?" asked Robert.

Longerst replied, "The thief is far from here. He robbed us all and buried the entire Zephyr Village. I am accompanying you to stop him. The spirit of zinc was sent by him to kill us."

Lightbuster said, "I think we must go to the Caves of Destiny. We will come to know what will happen in his path."

On the way, the three friends took a rest at a place known as the 'Atlantic Plateau'. They spent the night there. In the morning, they left for the 'Mountain of Heroics'. This was where Lightbuster wanted to go. On the tip of the mountain, were the Caves Of Destiny.

THE HIDDEN PROPHECY

At dawn, they reached the Mountain Of Heroics. The mountain was divided into three halves: *Armoury, Atlantic Orange Desert,* and *Caves Of Destiny.* There was also a lift. Two security guards gave them a murderous look. There was a snap and they stopped staring at them.

Robert was dazzled by the sunlight coming from the glass in the Caves Of Destiny. Yes, they were at the top of the Heroic Mountain.

Robert asked Lightbuster, "Is this the place where you wanted to come to ?"

"No", said Lightbuster.

There were plenty of shelves. They were filled with prophecies. On-shelf 408, they found Robert's prophecy. It was hidden behind a broken sharded prophecy.

A green mist came out and said,

"O! Robert O! Robert!"

"You'll succeed but shall be betrayed. The dark will reign in the end. But you will live!!"

THE GENIE OF KRIULEM

Before the suspense could break, there was a wide blast that broke Robert's prophecy. A man in black robes was curiously looking into the broken prophecy and sniggering at the three friends. Lightbuster knew he had to do something. A wide variety of prophecies had been stolen by the man.

He said, "The prophecy that you just heard was fake. The real prophecy is with my brother Robinson. He will be able to help."

Before he could complete his sentence, Lightbuster shot a silver knife into the man's stomach, killing him.

"Why did you do that?", Longerst asked angrily, "Are you crazy? Robinson was an old friend of mine. So, if this guy was his brother, then you have killed one of my friend's relatives."

"NOTHING!", Lightbuster said and walked away casually. Robert and Longerst exchanged a dark look as Lightbuster walked away.

Now, they had surpassed the Mountain Of Heroics and their next destination was 'Zephyr Village Caves'. They entered the first cave and saw total darkness in front of them. Suddenly a light flickered brightly making the cave visible. It was a lamp.

Lightbuster was about to pick it up when Longerst pulled it away. Robert had seen lamps in Aladdin. But a real lamp? It seemed impossible. Longerst rubbed the lamp. A thick paste oozed out of the lamp and out came a genie.

The thing was that the genie was evil.

It spoke in a reptilian voice, "I am the genie of Kriulem. It is this valley beyond the sixth cave. The thief sent me here to destroy you."

He threw a sword at Robert, who cut the blade with his zinc one. The genie turned the cave into an icy camp with huge crystals that blocked the way. A dozen arrows shot from beyond the crystals, slicing them and disintegrating the monster.

THE CITY

It was a scientist, judging by the looks of him. He wore a green shirt with a bit of confetti on him. He had a batch that said, *Confron*. Robert thought that it was his name because he later introduced himself by the same name.

He took them to his small hut in the next cave. He did this because he and the heroes became friends. The scientist was very intelligent and devised a plan to make them escape.

Confron said, "The other four caves are deadly and therefore we will travel through this trapdoor".

He indicated towards the trapdoor next to his bookshelf.

"After we have traveled underground, we will reach a flight of steps that will take us to Kriulem - the city of Monsters", he continued.

Robert asked Confron, "But how will we get to the place where the actual prophecy is?"

Confron said, "After visiting Kriulem, we will have to go to the thief's hideout where the prophecy is, Robert.''

They began their journey at midnight under the trapdoor. The journey was very long and took several days. When they had reached Kriulem, it was April 30, XY75. They just had a month to finish the quest.

After reaching Kriulem, they fought many monsters and genies and did not touch anything, due to Confron's warnings.

The first monster was Priondo. He looked a bit like a potato on the head. He fought them for like 10 minutes before Longerst cut his head off.

The last monster that they faced was another genie. This time with a THUD! Robert defeated the genie in a minute.

On May 6, XY75, Robert, Longerst, Lightbuster, and Confron reached the thief's hideout. They saw many things. Robert noticed a prophecy at the center of the hideout.

He tried to reach out but was stopped by an invisible force. A dark voice filled the room.

It said, "Robert, you think you can get to the prophecy? I am the thief of Zephyr and will kill you in the end. Ha! Ha! Ha! Find me before I destroy you."

A rope shot from the ceiling taking away the prophecy. Robert tried to stop it but was stopped by some monsters in black robes.

THE ARMY OF DESERTHOLDERS

There were at least seven ugly brown beetles just like the desertholder in 'The caves of Doom'. They fought a huge battle. The monsters kept on attacking. Finally, Robert killed a desertholder, taking away the electric axe from him. He threw the axe on the other desertholders killing them. Robert banged the axe on the table. The force blocking them cracked apart.

Robert told the other three friends, "I and Longerst shall follow the path of the ceiling while Confron and Lightbuster will follow the trapdoor", he pointed to a rusty bronze door.

Soon, they went to their own assigned destinations.

THE MONSTERS OF 3 DOORS

Robert and Longerst jumped on the table. Robert used his axe to slice the wood and make a ceildoor.

Upon reaching above the door, they had to fight four monsters that guarded three bronze metal doors. Next to the metal doors was a flight of steps that was latched. Robert killed two monsters and told Longerst to kill the others. Longerst took knives that he carried and threw them straight on the monsters' chests.

Robert and Longerst tried to read the doors but couldn't read them because there were misspelled words etched on the doors. Above the three doors was a big headline that said **The 3 Sourtsnom Srood**. Robert saw through the holes and saw nothing but monsters and then realized that it was **The 3 Monstrous Doors**.

Robert realized that they had to go through the flight of steps. He threw his axe on the latched doors of the steps. The axe broke, taking the doors with it.

THE CUP OF JAVA

Meanwhile, Lightbuster and Confron went down an alley after going under the trapdoor. They kept walking for hours and hours.

By 10 PM, they had walked for 6 hours and killed 3 monsters. Suddenly, a monster popped out from above. He threw his blades. Confron, the scientist defended himself and murdered the monster. He found a treasure box and saw that it was a dead-end. He opened the box and found a cup that said *Java*.

Before Confron could speak, Lightbuster threw a blade that caught Confron in the chest.

Lightbuster said, "You are so foolish. Do you think that you can take that? That cup is the only key to save Zephyr village and if I steal the Java city, then Zephyr will get over and all of the villagers will die."

Lightbuster laughed and said as a farewell, "Die alone, Confron. Vale!"

Confron choked and fell to the ground, clutching his throat in an attempt to remove the poison.

Meteorex, Lightbuster's father, lived in the Valley of Zinc and felt a disturbing twist in his son. He flew to where he had felt a strange disturbance: to Confron.

He healed Confron through his green potion that he carried for emergencies. Confron told Meteorex how Lightbuster had twisted to the dark side and escaped - surprisingly without the cup of Java.

"My son has dark traits.", Meteorex said with a sigh. "Now come on. We need to warn your friends before it's too late."

THE SHIP

Robert and Longerst climbed the flight of steps. They had reached a large deck full of ships. It was the terrace of the hideout.

They found a ship and jumped into the ship. It said *Tributer*. A snap and Meteorex and Confron stood next to the ship.

Confron asked, "Shall we take another ship?"

"Yes! Hang on, where's Lightbuster?" Robert asked.

Confron said, "We'll explain later."

After they were in the ships, they took off.

On the way, Longerst said, "Robert, hold the controls".

Robert found the place where the thief was. They sped off in that direction. It was at the end of Zephyr city. The Zephyr village is just a part of a city.

The entire city is known as Zephyr city. Anyway, it was at the cliff of the city. A place covered with lava.

They made a safe landing. Meteorex and Confron explained what had happened under the trapdoor. The date was May 8, XY75. A peal of cold laughter echoed through the hall.

It said, "Ha! You Fools! You can never defeat me. Give me the cup of Java and I will let you escape".

MAGNETISATION OF JAVA

It was the thief. He sent an army of desertholders. There was a very long battle, lasting for five days and twenty hours. Suddenly, Lightbuster arrived, stopped Robert, and tried to kill him. Lightbuster bound Robert and Confron, throwing them in a dungeon.

Meanwhile, Longerst and Meteorex were fighting monsters. Lightbuster threw two blades at Longerst, who defended himself.

"Not this time, Foolish Light!" He threw a blade at the top of a volcano destroying Light.

The thief was still alive. He fought with Meterox while Longerst was almost dead. He didn't give up. They fought for 10 more days. It was June 2, XY75. They had to escape. They had only one day to get the thief.

Under the trapdoor, a monster's voice echoed. Confron cut his and

Robert's ropes. The monster attacked them and they fought with all their might. The monster got defeated but ran away with the cup of Java.

Longerst fought with the thief and bound him. They had to reach Zephyr Village as soon as possible.

Meanwhile, Robert and Confron followed the monster to get the cup out of the monster's hands. It could save Zephyr village. They tossed around. Robert jumped on the monster and killed it with the zinc sword. Confron took the cup and followed the steps out of the dungeon.

A sword fell and it was the death of five desertholders by Longerst. Confron and Robert came out of the dungeon.

Robert, Meteroex, Confron, and Longerst pulled the thief by the scruff of this neck and sat in their spaceship. They destroyed the entire place which melted. When they were about to take off, the cup of Java fell.

Immediately greenery, mountains, and lots and lots of rivers were formed. There were fertile places and underground places. The cliff broke and the city fell. The water melted and the city stayed there forever. It was the city of Java.

The magnetisation had taken place. The entire river vaporized and was covered by the city. There were huts and about fifty men in the city. A village elder was standing in front of the city. Robert told them to land on Java,

The village elder said, "Well done! Your work is done. The cure shall be prosecuted and Zephyr village shall be healed. You don't have time, only 4 more hours!"

THE CURE

Once they were in *Tributer*, Confron said, "We'll speed at lightspeed. We shall reach Zephyr village in two hours."

Meanwhile, during the flight, Robert asked Meteorex, "Anyway, what happened to the prophecy about me and who is Lightbuster exactly?"

Meteorex replied, "The prophecy was smashed at the volcanic place by Lighbuster.

Robert! Lightbuster is the leader of all the Desertholders, not just the invaders. He's immortal and can be stopped by a magic item, which shall destroy him forever."

The thief stirred in his dreams as he had fainted.

Soon, they had reached Zephyr village. *Tributer* crashed exactly in front of the Celestial building, where Robert and Longerst had become friends. They jumped out of the ship. Suddenly, a white beam shot from Java.

Happiness spread everywhere and it stopped snowing. The mist from the building turned into a man.

He said, "Excellent work! Now, we shall execute the thief, shouldn't we?"

Robert turned to see two villagers tying the thief. Soon he was cut and that was the end of the thief. He was dead. Victory had taken place.

A ZEPHIRITE LIE

After their victory, they rejoiced. A party was celebrated until the end of the day.

The man who had given Robert the task said, "Robert, except for you, no other hero has ever returned alive from the thief's hideout. No prophecy concerns you. Who broke that fake prophecy?"

"Lightbuster did it", Robert said, "Which is the key that can be used to kill Lightbuster forever?"

The man said, "Child, the key is in a place that we have not yet explored. If Lightbuster dies, the desertholders will end."

Robert asked one more thing. "One last thing. What is your name? And.. uh... "

"My name is Robinson. And my brother was killed by Lightbuster. That's a mystery.."

Robert didn't understand and walked away. He was happy now that the village was cured and everyone was satisfied. June

XY75 passed. Now that his adventure was over, he had to go home for scientific works.

On July 1, XY75, Robert went outside in the snow to have a last look around Zephyr Village before departure. Before he could, however, the Earth started rumbling and with an earth-shattering BOOM, two desertholders appeared.

HAPPY BIRTHDAY ROBERT

The two ugly desertholders stared at Robert. He called for help. Robinson and others arrived at his help. They destroyed the monsters and then tracked the signal down to the singer of marshmallows.

"A new quest! You three need to go and track down the singer of marshmallows and kill him because I have good reason to believe that he's gonna send a few more monsters. And by the way,

Robert, HBD.", Robinson said, "We could find the singer hopefully in Java.

The analyses and surveys took a month.

Confron had gone back to his house. Robert and Longerst had to go get him. So, after a hasty birthday celebration of Robert (11) and giving him a hammer for a birthday gift, the two departed for Kriulem.

TRAVELLING TO THE CAVES

Robert thought of getting Confron back for this new quest. It would be best for him.

Robert remembered his ship: TRIBUTER. It was near the docking stands. He jumped into it with Longerst behind.

"Where is Confron?", Robert asked.

Longerst answered, "He is on his way to his house in the cave trying to destroy Kriulem as it is infested with the most dangerous monsters.

Meanwhile, Lightbuster is- "OK!", Robert cut Longerst short. "I will go and get Confron then." TRIBUTER landed right in front of the second cave where Confron lived. Touchdown!

Robert ran to Confron's small hut. What he saw was weird.

Confron sat on his chair reading a book with one leg hanging in mid-air and the other stable on the ground. His clothes were tattered. And he was eating a muffin. Yet, when Robert walked in he spoke as casually as he could: "Hello Robert. Have a seat."

Robert sat on the sofa and said, "I haven't come here to take your uh.. hospitality. I have arrived here to tell you about our new quest."

Robert explained to Confron everything that Robinson had said about the singer of marshmallows. "Good! So you want me to come on this quest? OK!", Confron replied.

After a few minutes, the two of them left the house. As if someone was watching, right on cue, Confron's house exploded, knocking Robert and Confron across the cave.

THE RETURN OF LIGHTBUSTER

WHO COULD IT BE other than Lightbuster?

Lightbuster was wearing a black hood today with a sword as long as his arm. He was also carrying a spare dagger in his pocket. "Surprise! OLD friends!" Then he noticed them both unconscious, "OOPS! Tie them and search for the third musketeer."

Luckily, Longerst had already noticed Lightbuster and his ship coming down the hill and therefore hidden away in the bushes. Lightbuster sent two desertholders to look for Longerst. Longerst jumped right in front of them and with a splat killed them off.

All Longerst now had to do was to save Robert and Confron. But luck was not on Longerst's side. He could hear Lightbuster laughing with binoculars pointing at him.

"Hello Longerst", said the evil mastermind and threw ropes around Longerst.

THE EVIL REQUEST

By now, Robert had woken up and was ready to go from these miserable caves. He removed his hammer from his pocket quietly unraveling his ropes and threw his hammer. It went across the caves killing the desertholders and punching Lightbuster in the face and then returning to Robert's hands.

"Did it hurt?", Robert asked Lightbuster.

"You have been trained well", Lightbuster said. "Due to that I have an offer for you: Join Me. Stop being a nobody. These Zephirites have covered your mind giving you quests. You are better off with me and the desertholders. I will give you anything you want after you join me: Power, Weaponry, Armour, Immortality - you name it! So what do you have to say?"

Robert answered, "Nope! I refuse".

"Huh", Lightbuster said, "If that's the case then... Monopoly!"

A green man with 45 bags of loot and 5 guns in his pocket appeared. "Yes Sir!"

"Kill them!", Lightbuster said smiling.

THE RUNAWAY THREE

Lightbuster disappeared. "Coward!", Robert thought and faced Lightbuster's supposed monster. Then he remembered his friends. They were no more unconscious. They were stuck in the ropes. Robert freed them up and began fighting Monopoly in a vigorous battle. While he was fighting, the caves started shaking.

"Get the ship ready, Confron and Longerst", Robert said while fighting. The two ran.

Robert fought and fought until... he cracked Monopoly's sword into two, but left him alive. Robert was tired of people dying due to Lightbuster. He sheathed his hammer and walked back to TRIBUTER, which had been readied by Longerst and Confron.

"Monopoly! Come on.", Robert told Monopoly.

"No. Never. I will stay here and you should too. I name you the Runaway 3." Robert looked stunned.

Suddenly, the ground started cleaving into two. Monopoly fell and died. The caves started falling. Robert jumped into TRIBUTER just as the ship started flying in midair.

THE DEMISE

Once on the ship, the trio was safe. Confron mourned the loss of his house. Longerst was driving TRIBUTER and Robert was thinking how Lightbuster could've let them go so easily.

After a while, Longerst said, "We are nearing Java."

This cheered Robert up. He was excited to revisit Java and as their quest was there, what was there not to feel excited about in Java.

As they were about to land a metal went CLANG! And the ship started to go in the opposite direction, into the Sea Of Nothingness. Longerst started changing direction. Robert looked outside the window and noticed Lightbuster's ship. It seemed that he had struck them down and in a second, Light's ship disappeared.

"Lightbuster: AGAIN.", Robert said, "We have to jump."

"Alright!", Confron and Longerst said.

Longerst let go of the controls and together the three of them jumped straight on the hard rocky surface of Java. On the other hand, TRIBUTER crashed into the Nothing Sea exploding into a billion pieces.

WELCOME BACK

Robert was welcomed enthusiastically by the village headman. Robert decided to take a break there. They hadn't even realized but the date was August 3, XY75: 2 days after they had left Zephyr Village.

Living in Java was a glamorous pleasure. Robert looked at the young children playing on the swings made of gold; the forges sparkling peacefully, the chocolate weapon to kill Lightbuster, etc. etc...

On 5th August XY75, Robert realized why he had come here with his two friends and asked the village headman where the singer of marshmallows was.

The village headman answered," I don't know much about the singer of marshmallows. But there is someone who would know."

THE 16 TRAPDOORS

After getting the advice from the village headman, Robert, Longerst, and Confron started searching for 'Blood After Blood', the vampire who supposedly knew all about the singer of marshmallows. Unfortunately, Blood After Blood used to roam around the 16 trapdoors located underneath the forge. Therefore, nobody knew where that vampire was at a given point in time.

Robert, Longerst, and Confron's job were to search for him in the sixteen trapdoors. Early morning of 6th August XY75, they began the hunt. Robert, Longerst, and Confron went from uh... Trapdoor to trapdoor searching for Blood After Blood but they couldn't find him.

After searching for three days, Longerst gave up. "Are you sure this is going to work? We are wasting time. The singer is sending one after another desertholder at our city and we are scrounging for a *vampire.*"

"OK!", Robert answered sarcastically, "Let us look for the singer of marshmallows without anyone's help."

As Confron calmed the two of them down, a hissing voice erupted from the 16th trapdoor.

"There!", Confron said and the trio went to the 16th trapdoor to meet Blood After Blood, the great vampire.

BLOOD AFTER BLOOD

After bounding into the last trapdoor, they saw the most gruesome sight ever. A vampire was standing with blood all over his face, a knife in his left hand and a sickly looking right hand. He wore a permanent scowl and had crisp black hair.

"HELLO! I am Blood After Blood. Nice to meet you.", said the vampire excitedly, "Are you on my lunch course?"

Robert answered, "Uh... No. We have come here to know more about the singer of-" The vampire cut him short "Marshmallows. Hmmm. They are tasty. Anyway: Yes, I shall provide you with the information you need but in exchange for a favor."

Robert did not want any more side quests but he couldn't refuse a vampire unless he wanted his skull raked into tiny little pieces by Blood After Blood. Hmm...

Suddenly, he got an idea: he could send Confron on whatever side quest Blood After Blood was giving while they got the information on the singer of marshmallows.

WOW! Blood After Blood agreed to the deal and soon Confron was on his way on the quest, whatever it was.

"Robert and Longerst", the vampire said, "I am usually good at the blood. You could be tasty treats. But, the singer of marshmallows lives in a place called Dark Cliffs. This place is right next to The Thief's Hideout and you know where that is." Robert and Longerst understood what the vampire was trying to say.

SIDEQUEST!!!

Confron thought that the side quest would be easy peasy. Just save a bunny rabbit from underneath another of the trapdoors. But he couldn't even find that trapdoor.

Confron took an hour and a half to search for this little rabbit. The rabbit was hanging at the end of a corner. And it fell straight into a pool. Confron had no choice and jumped in the pool too.

Confron swam after the rabbit and finally caught him and tried to haul him back to the 16th trapdoor. But the rabbit started shouting.

"OK kid. Quiet. Your big friend Blood After Blood told me to save you.", Confron said to the rabbit.

At the words 'Blood After Blood,' the rabbit ran up the water and went running to the 16th trapdoor with Confron running behind him." Oh Yes", Blood After Blood said and gobbled up the rabbit.

"Ugh!", Confron said, "I thought that was your friend."

"Friend. Yeah. By the way, your friends have gone to the Dark Cliffs."

EXTINCTION

Robert and Longerst had darted to a new ship (with TRIBUTER in repairs). Then they had run off to the Dark Cliffs.

The Dark Cliffs were cliffs drifting in the sky, weirdly enough and they were right next to the Thief's Hideout or its ruins anyway.

After landing on the Dark Cliffs, a hissing noise came out of the ground and a snake slithered out right from under the ground.

Robert killed off the snake with his hammer. As he did, another wave of snakes slithered out of the ground. They were hopelessly outnumbered.

The first sign of help was that golden ship. And then, Confron skillfully shot down every single snake before it could even come out of the ground. The snakes had come to extinction.

THE RED BOLTER

After walking for a while, the trio spotted an enormous castle. They entered it with a Clang! And they met their challenge.

The guard was 6 feet tall. The Red Bolter. Blood After Blood had warned them about him. Lightbuster had set up good measures but luckily Robert knew how to kill this guy.

Robert fought Red courageously with a thunderous battle. In the end, Robert finished the battle with a last bolt of lightning from his lightning.

GAME OVER For the red bolter.

THE LAST MARSHMALLOW

Once inside, the trio found the singer of marshmallows sitting on a throne. He saw them and then rose to end them once and for all. Robert regained his hammer, Longerst steadied his sword, Confron got ready with a gun. They attacked at the same time.

Robert cut through all of the marshmallows that were turning into desertholders. Confron cut off the singer's hand. Longerst fought bravely. Then, Robert jumped and cut off the singer's head triumphantly.

Suddenly, two heads appeared on the singer's neck. Sort of like the …. Hydra. Robert thought about that greek myth. But the idea was ridiculous. Had the greek myths come alive now?

"Ha!", the singer said as if he could read Robert's mind.

"I was created by Lightbuster to resemble the Hydra. But the problem is I can live only twice."

"Ha!", Robert suddenly said, "Never announce your secret weakness." He jumped and lopped off the two heads of the singer.

"NO!", the singer wailed and burst into a million pieces, shattering the whole palace. The trio somehow managed to run. They got into the golden ship as the entire Dark Cliffs exploded and crashed down on top of Thief's Hideout.

"Another ruin.", said Robert jokingly. Victory!!

After reaching Zephyr Village on 9th August XY75, Robert was given special awards for his bravery. He went back home, promising Robinson that he'll be back next time they need him to save the day. Everyone was happy. Well... not Lightbuster.

QUESTERMOLOGY

10 August, XY75.

Lightbuster was angry as he sat in his ship hovering in midair.

"Killed! How can he just be killed?", he roared with anger at the desertholder who had gotten him the news of the marshmellow's death.

"Sir... I don't know. We think it is Robert.", the poor guy replied.

Lightbuster shot a bolt of lightning at the desertholder and zapped him into ashes.

"Get me a new sword. I am off on a quest to get the most fearful monster of all.", Lightbuster ordered his desertholders. "It is time to get Dracula. The longest and the most horror story ever will return….".

INTRODUCTION TO DRACULA

Lightbuster started narrating the story of Dracula - the story that had been told a dozen billion times across the world.

"Dracula: The evilest monster. The first reincarnation of Dracula was created by the GREAT SCULPTOR in the year XY54 as a key to destroy the world. He'd been constructing this tool for a decade. The moment Dracula had been constructed, he killed the old sculptor. He escaped Zephyr

Village and fled to the real world via a trapdoor. The reincarnation was destroyed soon by the hands of a Zephirite. The second reincarnation had formed and gone back to Zephyr Village, hidden in disguise. He was caught in the year XY63, eleven years after he had created this second incarnation. He was thrown back to the mortal world and the third reincarnation of Dracula went hidden underneath a giant tree in the mortal world, from where he started killing humans one by one. It is said that he is now in his fifth reincarnation with the information of the fourth reincarnation lost to the world. And now, it's my job to find him and this time I will."

Lightbuster packed his bags and headed for an escape pod. He jumped into it and the escape pod took off.

Lightbuster fidgeted with his controls and said, "To Dracula - The greatest vampire"...

EPILOGUE

A Continuation To The Upcoming Book

Mr.Cyber hated being a computer engineer. First of all, he had to build a huge robot for Toybag's exclusive, why - he had no idea. Then he was asked to design a videogame for people who had got diseases. He had sympathized and therefore given in. Yet, that wasn't it, was it?

Mr.Cyber woke up late on 11 August XY75, thinking that today he might learn something new from coding! As he got up, his phone started vibrating...

"No more phone calls, please!", he said to himself.

He picked up the phone.

"Hello?", he said lazily to whoever was on the other line.

"It is time to come back", said a familiar voice.

"Robinson?", he said amazed.

"Yes! It's me. Now come on. We need your help, engineer.", Robinson answered.

"At your service", Cyber said and darted towards the trapdoor that had long been covered with books and computers.

He tossed everything aside, wore a silver jacket with a silver MAC, and jumped thru the trapdoor...

AND...

To be continued...

COMING IN 2021
Javians & Zephirites
Book Two
The Never-Ending Catastrophe

MAP

FROM NORMAL WORLD → 20 KMS AWAY →XYOSTER CITY

XYOSTER CITY → 10 KMS INSIDE → ROBERT'S HOME

ROBERT'S HOME → TRAPDOOR → ZEPHYR VILLAGE

ZEPHYR VILLAGE → SOME MILES AWAY → ZEPHYR VALLEY CAVES

ZEPHYR VALLEY CAVES → DEEPER → KRIULEM

KRIULEM → LITTLE AWAY → THIEF'S HIDEOUT

THIEF'S HIDEOUT → DARK CLIFFS
DARK CLIFFS → AWAY → THE SEA OF NOTHINGNESS

THE SEA OF NOTHINGNESS → 1 KM AWAY → JAVA

JAVA → THE 16 TRAPDOORS

ABOUT THE AUTHOR

Armaan Bhimani is an Indian-American author. He is a 13 year old who has been passionate about books and an avid reader since childhood. Armaan is a Spellbee Champ at various levels. He loves reading both fiction as well as non-fiction books. He spends most of his time either reading books or writing short stories.

While this is his first book, Armaan's next book is already on it's way.

For more information on Armaan Bhimani and his books follow theauthorarmaan.wordpress.com or write to him at theauthorarmaan@gmail.com.

Made in the USA
Columbia, SC
21 December 2020